Dear Parent:
Your child's love of reading starts here!

Every child learns to read in a different way and at his or her own speed. Some go back and forth between reading levels and read favorite books again and again. Others read through each level in order. You can help your young reader improve and become more confident by encouraging his or her own interests and abilities. From books your child reads with you to the first books he or she reads alone, there are I Can Read Books for every stage of reading:

SHARED READING
Basic language, word repetition, and whimsical illustrations, ideal for sharing with your emergent reader

BEGINNING READING
Short sentences, familiar words, and simple concepts for children eager to read on their own

READING WITH HELP
Engaging stories, longer sentences, and language play for developing readers

READING ALONE
Complex plots, challenging vocabulary, and high-interest topics for the independent reader

ADVANCED READING
Short paragraphs, chapters, and exciting themes for the perfect bridge to chapter books

I Can Read Books have introduced children to the joy of reading since 1957. Featuring award-winning authors and illustrators and a fabulous cast of beloved characters, I Can Read Books set the standard for beginning readers.

A lifetime of discovery begins with the magical words "I Can Read!"

Visit www.icanread.com for information
on enriching your child's reading experience.

I Can Read Book® is a trademark of HarperCollins Publishers.

The Berenstain Bears and Mama for Mayor! Copyright © 2012 by Berenstain Publishing, Inc. All Rights Reserved. Manufactured in China. No part of this book may be used or reproduced in any manner whatsoever without written permission except in the case of brief quotations embodied in critical articles and reviews. For information address HarperCollins Children's Books, a division of HarperCollins Publishers, 10 East 53rd Street, New York, NY 10022.
www.icanread.com

Library of Congress catalog card number: 2011935481
ISBN 978-0-06-207528-4 (trade bdg.)—ISBN 978-0-06-207527-7 (pbk.)

12 13 14 15 16 SCP 10 9 8 7 6 5 4 3 2 1   ❖   First Edition

I Can Read!

BEGINNING 1 READING

The Berenstain Bears

and

MAMA FOR MAYOR!

B.C. TV

Jan & Mike Berenstain

HARPER

An Imprint of HarperCollins*Publishers*

Clunk!

The Bear family's car hit a hole in the road.

Bump!

The car hit a bump in the road.

"Someone should do something
about this road,"
said Mama.
"Yes," said Papa. "But who?"

Back home, Mama thought and thought.

"I know what to do to fix the road,"
she said. "I will run for mayor!"
"Good idea," said Papa.
"Hooray!" cried the cubs.
"Mama for mayor!"

So Mama went to the town hall
to sign up to run for mayor.
Papa, Brother, Sister, and Honey
went with her.
They were going to help her run for mayor.

The whole family made posters that said "Mama for mayor."

They put them up around town.

The family made buttons, shirts, and hats
that said "Mama for mayor."
They put them on and wore them
around town.

Papa put up signs on their car.

He drove around town shouting

"Mama for mayor!"

13

All the bears running for mayor
went to the town hall.
They gave speeches.
Mama listened to the speeches.
She thought they were
pretty boring.

Mama gave her speech.

She said she would fix the roads.

Everyone cheered.

She said she would put up

new streetlights.

Everyone cheered.

GO MAMA!

YES!

AWESOME!

Mama liked it when everyone cheered.

She said she would get the trash

picked up.

Everyone cheered.

"Dear," whispered Papa, "maybe you are

saying too much."

But Mama went right on.

Mama said there would be honey
in every pot.
She said there would be salmon
in every stream.
All the bears cheered and stomped
and whistled.
"Mama for mayor!" they shouted.

The day to vote soon came.

Mama and Papa voted early.

So did the other bears running for mayor.

22

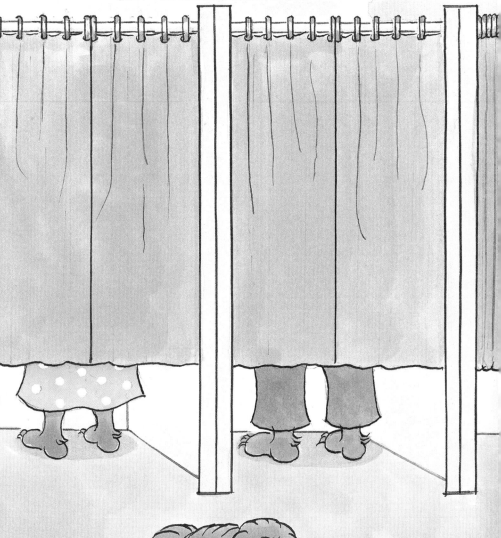

Mama went to The Burger Bear
for breakfast.
She shook hands.
She kissed babies.
She posed for pictures.

Mama, Papa, and the cubs went home.

They waited for the votes to be counted.

Later, they heard shouting outside.

"Hooray!" they heard. "Mama wins!"

Mama was the new mayor of Bear Country.

She went to sleep very happy.

But the next morning,

Mama was not so happy.

There was a big crowd

outside the tree house.

They were angry.

They carried signs and shouted.

"Fix the road!" they shouted.

"Put up streetlights!" they yelled.

"Pick up the trash!" they called.

They wanted Mayor Mama to do
all the things she said she would—
right now!

"There is just one thing wrong with running for mayor," said Brother. "You just might win!"